Duck In A Bowtie

E.S.Gleason

Ukiyoto Publishing

All global publishing rights are held by

Ukiyoto Publishing

Published in 2022

Content Copyright © E.S.Gleason

ISBN 9789360161712

All rights reserved.
No part of this publication may be reproduced, transmitted, or stored in a retrieval system, in any form by any means, electronic, mechanical, photocopying, recording or otherwise, without the prior permission of the publisher.

The moral rights of the author have been asserted.

This is a work of fiction. Names, characters, businesses, places, events, locales, and incidents are either the products of the author's imagination or used in a fictitious manner. Any resemblance to actual persons, living or dead, or actual events is purely coincidental.

This book is sold subject to the condition that it shall not by way of trade or otherwise, be lent, resold, hired out or otherwise circulated, without the publisher's prior consent, in any form of binding or cover other than that in which it is published.

www.ukiyoto.com

Dedicated to my wonderful Son Carter
And to
Shannon and Brendan's adorable Baby Boy
Ashton Ross Galloway

Contents

Learn to Count with Our Animal Friends with a Fun	1
One Yellow Duck With a Red bowtie.	3
Two Pink Pigs in Polka Dot Boots.	4
Three Turtles in Top Hats.	5
Four Salamanders with Shades, Sunning Themselves.	6
Five Frogs in Feathered hats.	7
Six Spotted Snails.	8
Seven Slithering Stripped Snakes.	9
Eight Kittens with Kites.	10
Nine Swimming Sharks.	11
Ten Grazing Cows.	12
Eleven Busy Bumble Bees.	13
Twelve Bouncing Kangaroos.	14
Thirteen Lounging Leopards.	15
Fourteen Carpenter Ants.	16
Fifteen Penguins with Purple Purses.	17
Great Job! Now let's Count all the Way to Fifteen.	18
You did Amazing, way to go!	19

About the Author   *20*

Learn to Count with Our Animal Friends with a Fun

1 2 3

For added fun, can you find Steve the squirrel on every page?

Steve the Squirrel

One Yellow Duck With a Red bowtie

Two Pink Pigs in Polka Dot Boots.

Three Turtles in Top Hats.

Four Salamanders with Shades, Sunning Themselves.

Five Frogs in Feathered hats.

Six Spotted Snails.

Seven Slithering Stripped Snakes.

Eight Kittens with Kites.

Nine Swimming Sharks.

Ten Grazing Cows.

Eleven Busy Bumble Bees.

Twelve Bouncing Kangaroos.

Thirteen Lounging Leopards.

Fourteen Carpenter Ants.

Fifteen Penguins with Purple Purses.

Great Job! Now let's Count all the Way to Fifteen.

You did Amazing, way to go!

About the Author

E.S.Gleason

E.S.Gleason is a resident of Michigan. He is currently working his way towards his Master's in Creative Writing and English. He credits his wonderful son Carter for the passion for writing and constant self-improvement. E.S.Gleason loves animals and all creepy crawly critters.

www.ingramcontent.com/pod-product-compliance
Lightning Source LLC
LaVergne TN
LVHW061628070526
838199LV00070B/6622